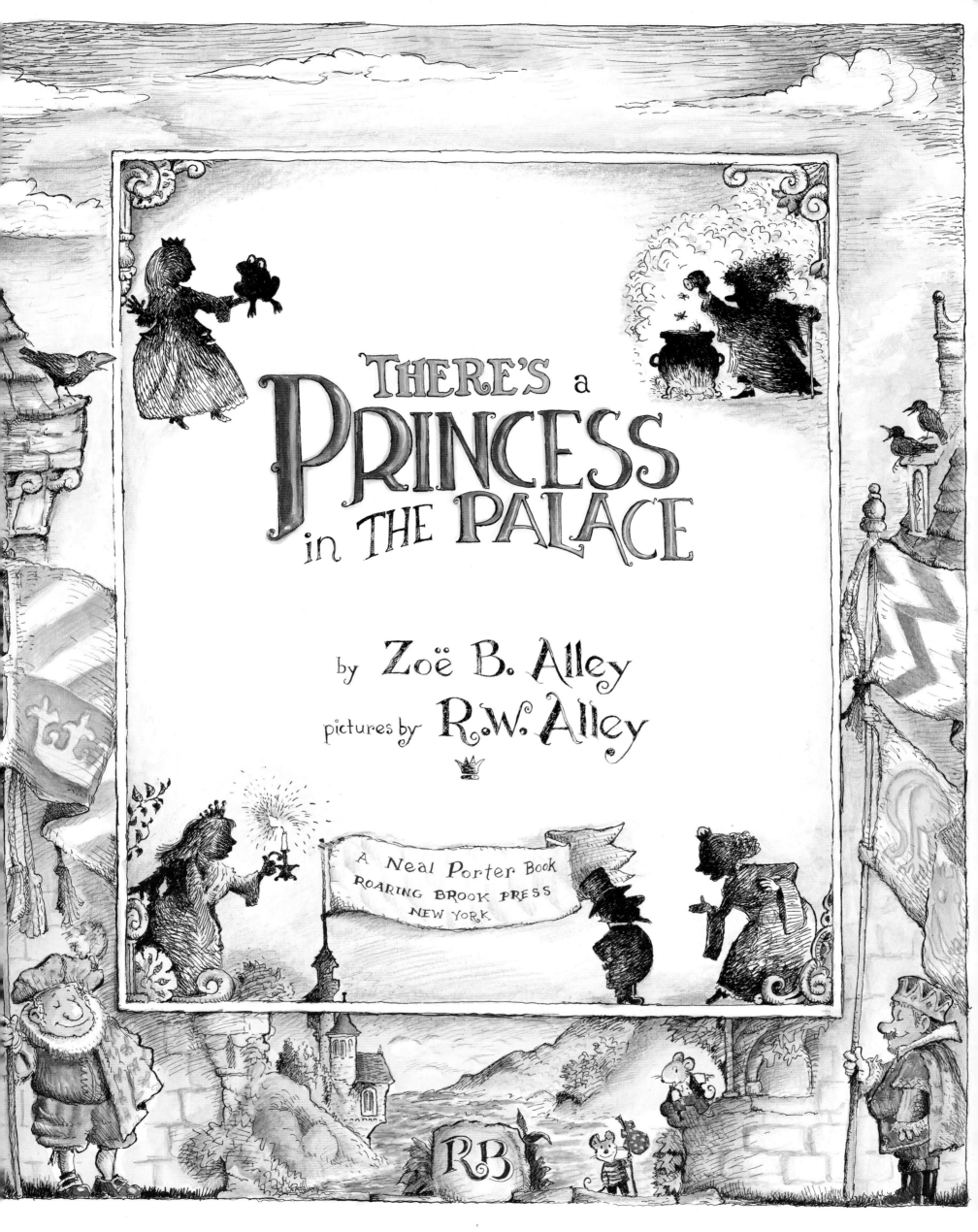

THERE'S a PRINCESS in THE PALACE

by Zoë B. Alley

pictures by R.W. Alley

A Neal Porter Book
ROARING BROOK PRESS
NEW YORK

Text copyright © 2010 by Zoë B. Alley

Illustrations copyright © 2010 by R.W. Alley

A Neal Porter Book

Published by Roaring Brook Press

Roaring Brook Press is a division of Holtzbrinck Publishing Holdings Limited Partnership

175 Fifth Avenue, New York, New York 10010

www.roaringbrookpress.com

Distributed in Canada by H. B. Fenn and Company Ltd.

Library of Congress Cataloging-in-Publication Data

Alley, Zoë B.

There's a princess in the palace / retold by Zoë B. Alley ; pictures by R.W. Alley. — 1st ed.

p. cm.

"A Neal Porter book."

Summary: Cinderella, Snow White, and three other well-known princesses share a surprising
connection in these fairy tale retellings presented in comic book format.

ISBN 978-1-59643-471-4

1. Graphic novels. [1. Graphic novels. 2. Princesses—Fiction. 3. Fairy tales. 4. Humorous stories.]
I. Alley, R. W. (Robert W.), ill. II. Title. III. Title: There is a princess in the palace.

PZ7.7.A38Th 2010

741.5'973]—dc22

2009042483

Roaring Brook Press books are available for special promotions and premiums.

For details contact: Director of Special Markets, Holtzbrinck Publishers.

First Edition September 2010

Book design by Jennifer Browne

Printed in May 2010 in China by South China Printing Co. Ltd., Dongguan City, Guangdong Province

1 3 5 7 9 8 6 4 2

Table of Contents

vi

Cinderella

Once upon a time in the Middle Ages, Cinderella was a wreck. Her widowed father had remarried a selfish and vain woman whose two daughters were as selfish and vain as she. Cinderella had been run ragged.

Where's my omelet, Cinderella?!

Cinderella! There's a *wrinkle* in my pillowcase! Do something!

How many times do I have to tell you—it's scrub, wash, iron, and *then* dust! Stupid girl!

Wow! The apple doesn't fall far from the tree, does it?

I think these are *crab* apples!

My father sure knows how to pick 'em!

Exhausted each morning from the previous day's workload, Cinderella often awoke by the fireplace hearth, lying among the soot and cinders. The name "Cinderella" stuck. So did the soot.

Look at you—what a mess! Have you no pride in your appearance, like us?

SNORT!

Could have been worse—she could have been called "Hearth-hunzel"!

Yes, that sure would have *grated* on me!

Meanwhile, in another part of the kingdom, the King and Queen decided it was time for their son—the Handsome Prince—to select a bride. Thinking a local maiden would be just the ticket, they decided to host a ball and invite all of the eligible maidens in the kingdom.

Don't I have any say in this?

Of course not! This is the 15th century!

Our son—such a comedian!

BREAKING NEWS

There Is a Young Prince—Hey! He's Single!
With Available Girls He Should Mingle!
Come One and Come All,
To the Big Royal Ball,
So That His Wedding Bells Soon May Jingle!

Oooh, a ball! How romantic!

Why couldn't they have had a *princess* instead?

Yeah, no one ever thinks about *our* needs!

I should get my nails done!

When the horrible stepsisters heard the announcement, they were thrilled. Each was convinced that the Handsome Prince would choose her.

Finally! Someone who will appreciate my quiet beauty!

Your beauty? No one holds a candle to my exquisiteness!

Girls, girls! Don't argue! It will give you gas

"Oh, Cinderella," teased the stepsisters, "don't you wish you could go to the ball?"
"Oh, yes!" agreed Cinderella dreamily. "Could I?"

The stepsisters shrieked with laughter.

Bra-ha! Don't be *stupid*, Cinderella! What would *you* wear to a ball? Go and get our best gowns ready!

Yes, and polish our tiaras, too!

Don't saunter, Cinderella! You must help the girls to look beautiful!

They'll certainly *need* the help!

And, a healthy imagination!

Overwhelmed with their beauty, the stepsisters and their loathsome mother left for the ball. "Have an absolutely *fabulous* evening," they called to Cinderella. "And don't forget the dishes!" Their laughs faded down the road with their carriage.

Cinderella sobbed over her suds.

Why are they always so mean to me? I wish chocolate cupcakes were invented—they would make me feel better!

You look like you could use a friend!

Cinderella's soapsuds flew everywhere.

"What the heck? Who are you?" said Cinderella, stunned. "I am your Fairy Godmother, of course," replied the fluttering Fairy Godmother. "How can I help you, sweetie?"

I didn't know this was a *fairy* tale!

Where did you *think* we were headed?

Cinderella recovered her wits and replied, "I just really want to go to the ball. I've never been anywhere, and I always look like something the cat dragged in!"

CAT?

Where? When did we get a cat?

"Well, I can surely grant you that wish, my dear! Shouldn't be too difficult," replied the Fairy Godmother. "Let's see, how about a pumpkin from the garden, please, that fine teddy bear of yours, and two little mice." "Of course, right away." responded the curious Cinderella.

Mice? Uh-oh!

I didn't realize this would require audience participation!

Cinderella gathered the items as she was told.

I protest!

My rights are being violated!

With a wave of her wand and a sprinkle of fairy dust, the Fairy Godmother poofed the pumpkin into a beautiful coach, turned the teddy into a handsome coachman, and morphed the mice into two gorgeous white horses.

Whoa!

That was wild!

You're not kidding!

I feel so powerful!

The Fairy Godmother smiled at her work. "Now, run along to the ball, honey! Have fun! Make good decisions!"

"But I can't go looking like *this*," replied Cinderella. "It wouldn't be proper."

"This always happens when I multitask— I really *must* pay more attention to detail!" said the Fairy Godmother, and she waved her wand once more. Cinderella looked down to behold the loveliest dress she could ever imagine, beautifully accessorized with a pair of elegant glass slippers.

Not very practical, though, are they?

No, but truly lovely!

Wow! I look amazing! And, my hair looks great! Thank you so much!

"Now, off you go," said the Fairy Godmother. "But remember, the magic only lasts until midnight. At the last stroke of twelve, all will be as it was before."

I'll remember! Let's go!

Phew! That's a relief! We won't be like this for long.

I don't know, I'm kind of into this large animal thing!

PALACE THIS EXIT

Once at the palace, guests buzzed about this newly arrived beauty.

But who is she?

Hello! This ball's looking up!

Where have we seen that face before?

4

Completely smitten with each other, the Handsome Prince and Cinderella danced every dance together and . . .

promptly fell deeply in love. So deeply, in fact, that Cinderella lost all track of time.

She heard the clock begin to strike twelve. Remembering her Fairy Godmother's words, Cinderella began to panic.

Oh no! I must leave! It's midnight!

No, wait! I don't even know your name! And, your shoe—you've dropped one—wait! Come back, whoever you are!

My shoes feel a little funny, too!

Too bad! I was just getting the hang of trotting!

As her coach sped away, Cinderella heard the last gong of the clock.

POOF!

The beautiful coach was a pumpkin once more, the handsome coachman a teddy bear, and Cinderella's lovely dress turned back to her old, tattered rags.

Oh no! There go the designer duds!

But what a lovely time I had!

Shouldn't the Prince love Cinderella no matter what she's wearing or who she is?

Of course, but she doesn't know that yet! The *moral* of the story comes at the end!

5

Of course, the slipper fit perfectly.

My princess! Marry me!

My prince! Okay!

My heavens! Her?

Guess it doesn't matter what you look like—it's what's *inside* that counts!

Ah, there's that *moral*!

On their wedding day, there was much happiness and rejoicing in the palace. The party went on well past midnight this time.

I'm so happy! Oh, my dear Cinder . . . Wait! Is that your *real* name?

No, my love! I'm so glad someone finally asked! It's "Ashley"!

I get it— *Cinder* and *Ash*!

What a long story for a bad pun!

LATER...

It's a Girl!

It's a girl!

It's a girl!

Congratulations Princess Ashley and Prince Dennis

I'm sorry, ma'am, but you're not on my list!

Don't you "ma'am" me, young man! And, how rude of them to overlook me! They will live to regret this oversight!

This way to see the baby.

Valet Parking

Uh-oh! This will probably have an effect on the other four stories!

Yeah, I'm thinking . . . "and they all lived happily ever after, until . . . !"

Oh, there once was a baby, brand new,
Whose folks overlooked me—boo-hoo!
A spell I will cast—
And long it will last!
They'll sleep for a decade or two!

Wow! What a witch!

She sure is annoying! No wonder she never gets invited to parties!

7

Sleeping Beauty

It's a Girl!

Once upon a time, Princess Dawn was a teenager.

Do you really expect me to wear this gown? It's *so* last season! And what's up with this room decor? Can't we at least *try* to be modern? Come on, people, get with the program!

Appealing, isn't she?

Mmmm—like a toothache!

Convinced that there must be more to the world than she beheld, Princess Dawn was antsy.

Dawn, sweetie, hurry! We'll be late for our morning stroll!

Must we always *stroll*? It seems so meaningless! Can't we maybe pick up the pace a bit? How about a good *saunter*?!

"Nothing new ever happens around here," moaned the frustrated Princess. "It's always the same Boring strolling, wandering, and overseeing! I'm so TIRED of it all!"

Why, honey, just last week you strolled from east to west, instead of west to east! *That* was exciting!

Daaaaaaad!

Nice whining!

Yes, very well done!

When I was her age, I was sweeping cinders out of fireplaces—but that's another story!

Tired of her miserable lot in life, Princess Dawn flew up the stairs to her favorite attic turret, and slammed the door.

There goes the plaster, again!

Guess I'll stroll alone!

Ahh, peace and quiet!

Annoyed beyond belief, Princess Dawn announced loudly—and to no one in particular—"It's So Boring around here that it's putting me to sleep!!!"

And down she went.

SLAM

Is she kidding?

I don't think so! Maybe it's that old woman's prophecy from the beginning of the story!

YAHOO! That spell worked like a charm!

Indeed, all over the castle, everything stopped. Servants snored at their tasks, meals ceased cooking, and the Royal Couple slumbered peacefully.

Why aren't *we* asleep?

Well, someone has to move the story along!

Time passed, and still the palace slept on. Thick vines grew up the walls and covered the castle. All that was visible was the very top of the turret where the now quiet Princess Dawn slumbered.

Wow, they must have *great* soil!

And some *crazy* fertilizer!

One day, a passing Handsome Prince stumbled upon the vine-covered palace. He was intrigued.

How intriguing!

There never seems to be a shortage of princes, does there?

No, and always handsome ones, too!

Feeling exceptionally brave and curious, he strode up to the gate. To his astonishment, the vines began to fall away in front of him, leading him slowly up the path to the castle door.

I'm feeling exceptionally brave and curious!

Oooh, I'd choose *panicked* and *scared*!

Absolutely!

Once inside the palace, the Handsome Prince was stunned to find the sleepy scene.

I'm stunned! What magic has befallen these sleepy sovereigns?

Oooh, fancy language!

Sure is! Guess he's well-bred as well as good looking!

The Prince made his way slowly through the castle, peering into rooms with curiosity.

10

All over the castle, things began to perk up. Startled servants rubbed their eyes and continued their chores. The King and Queen didn't skip a beat . . .

Better call the royal plasterer.

Time for my stroll—alone!

. . .while Princess Dawn was attempting to get to know her handsome admirer.

What are your goals for the future? Any diseases in your family? Like to try new things?

You're *lovely* when you're inquisitive! Be mine!

Oh brother, this guy's got it bad!

Yes, b[u]t h[e']d better give her some space! I do[n't] think she's ready fo[r] marriage[?] yet!

As the palace returned to life, the Princess, too, began to pick up where she left off. "Nice as you are," she declared firmly to the Prince, "you need to back off! I need to see the world before I settle down with *anyone*! I need an adventure!"

"I will explore the Woods," Princess Dawn announced to her concerned parents and doting Prince. "Don't try and stop me!"

But Honey Bun, you've never been past the palace gardens!

Oh, let her go! It will feel like a *vacation* without her!

Is she not the most *amazing* creature?!

Told you!

Guess a good night's sleep can only do *so* much!

Snow White and the Seven Dwarfs

Once upon a time, in the Woods, Princess Dawn knew she was lost.

Oh dear, it's all so disorienting in here! All this nature looks alike! I think I'm done with my adventure!

For goodness sake! She's only been gone ten minutes!

Do you think she should have taken the Beginners' trail in the last story?

So lost, in fact, that she grew scared. The Princess trembled. Her eyes filled up. She put on her best pout.

Well, *this* is annoying! I'm upset and there's no one here to help me! I hate to waste a good tantrum alone!

Wow! She really *does* look upset! She's even getting *pale*!

She sure is—as *white* as *snow*! Hey, I think we're on to something here! Shall we?

Oh, what the heck! It's good for the story!

"Snow White" considered her options. Although panicking was tops on her list, she chose instead to find a place to spend the soon-to-fall night.

Finally! A wise choice!

I can't shake the feeling that we're being followed!

I'd better make myself presentable, or she'll never fall for my next plan! I'll be sure that this one works— hey, is this thing on?

You betcha!

Finally, through a clearing, Snow White saw a cottage. Although tiny, it looked warm and inviting.

Les Lew Sam
Hank Nat
Myron Bethanne

She knocked. When there was no answer, Snow White tried the door. It wasn't locked. "Helloooo? It is I, your Princess!" called Snow White to the empty house. She went in. "I need a place to sleep and have selected your home! Helloooo?"

Doesn't she know that she should never enter a strange house?

Ooh, dinner. I'm starved!

Or, eat there!

As it grew dark, Snow White grew tired. "What a day I've had!" she yawned. "Being adventurous sure is exhausting! I'm sure that whoever lives here won't mind if royalty sleeps on their couch for tonight." She made herself comfy.

Wow, makes poor decisions, and *bossy*, too!

Yes, she's really the whole package!

Just as Snow White began some significant snoring, the cottage's actual owners returned home after a long day of shopping. The Dwarfs always found it difficult when they traveled anywhere together— there were so many of them—and they were sleepy, grumpy, and hungry.

Ach, such blisters!

You always wear the wrong shoes!

Can't you two be *quiet* already?!

Let's at least get in the door before you start!

Start? They've been *starting* for the last three blocks!

Well, you're no help!

OMG! Who is *that*?!

An intruder!

With a crown?

I told you to lock the door!

I'm scared!

Shhh, you'll wake her up!

She doesn't look dangerous!

I hope she's not a *thief*! I got some great bargains today!

No sooner had the Dwarfs left, than the Old Woman approached the cottage. She had spent an uncomfortable night in the Woods, but tried to pull herself together.

Mirror, Mirror, in my hand—
my back sure hurts! Can hardly stand!
But here I am at Snow White's door.
I'll try again, as I tried before!

What's with the cheesy rhyming?

The Old Woman rapped on the door. "Now what?" wondered Snow White to herself. "I'm hungry—can't a person grab a bite around here?" Opening the door, the Princess was startled. "Don't be afraid, my dear," said the Old Woman. "It is only me— a lovely, local farmer-woman—here to offer you a free sample from our recent crop. Welcome to the neighborhood!" And the Old Woman held out a beautiful, shiny apple to Snow White.

Wow, thanks! I'm starving! That's a great-looking apple, but you really could use some make-up tips!

Another bad decision: taking food from strangers!

I know, right? She just keeps 'em coming!

Eagerly, Snow White took a bite from the juicy apple. The last thing she heard before she fell to the floor was the Old Woman's cackle.

HA! That will teach your parents to leave me off their guest list!

Wow! She can really hold a grudge!

This sleep thing seems to be a pattern with her, doesn't it?

There went Snow White, down for the count! She was fast asleep once again. Thrilled, the Old Woman took her leave.

How brilliant am I?! *That* should hold her!

We really *should* talk lipstick shades! I think you're actually a "winter"!

"What fate has befallen my Princess?" exclaimed the worried Prince. "She looks so peaceful!"

It's getting crowded in here!

Looks can be deceiving!

We could always serve the apple!

Ooh, let's have a sleepover!

Next thing you know, we'll have the whole village!

There's that word again— befallen!

And no food in the house!

I told you we needed groceries!

Yes, isn't it funny how you never hear something, and then twice in one day!

Driven by impulse and concern, the Handsome Prince bent over the sleeping, snoring Snow White.
He gently kissed her on the forehead.

I am driven by impulse and concern!

Yes, yes, we know!

Snow White's eyelids began to flutter. Her snoring stopped. She opened one eye and looked around.

The Frog Prince

Are you sure you know what you're doing?

Just be quiet and *reflect*!

Oh, there **still** is that Princess—now grown—
Who has married, with child of her own!
So on her, I forebode—
She must love an old toad!
A **great** spell!
Or my name's not **Joan**!

I never knew that was your name!

I don't use it much!

Once upon a time, Princess Misty was morose.

Oh, no! My golden ball! I might as well be miserable!

At her age—playing with a *ball*? Shouldn't she be a bit more grown-up?

Oh, I don't know! Balls can be *fun*!

Whom is she talking to, anyway?

Good question! And in such long sentences!

Misty began to cry. Hard. "That ball was passed down to me from my grandmother, Princess Ashley!" she wailed. "It was a commemorative souvenir reminding her that she met Grandpa Dennis at a ball! And now it's gone!" Princess Misty made quite a scene.

Just as Misty began her slip into total despondency, she heard a voice. It appeared to be coming from the well itself. "What's that? Who's there?" called the startled, watery-eyed Princess.

22

Recovering her wits over talking to a slimy frog, Princess Misty told him of her crisis.

Whoa! Why all the fuss, Princess?

. . . And I'll get in *total* trouble for losing my family's ball! I'm not even supposed to be playing with it, but it's so shiny and pretty!

Well, no need to panic! I *am* a water creature, you know! And a *great* swimmer!

"If I help you," croaked the Frog, "What's in it for me?"

"Oh, wonderful Frog," replied the now-excited Princess, "I'll give you anything! I just don't want my parents to yell! They can make such a fuss over the smallest things!"

A fuss? Imagine!

Yes, sounds familiar!

The helpful Frog eagerly responded with his demands. "What I desire most in the world is to be treated with a little human kindness. Will you take me into your home and let me live as you do—eat at your table, sleep in a fluffy bed, hang out with you?"

Eeeeuuuw! A yucky frog in our nice, clean palace?!

I'm going to pretend I didn't hear that!

Her room certainly isn't nice and clean! Have you seen it lately?

I know, she's a royal slob!

But, try as she might to avoid the Frog's wishes, Princess Misty realized she needed help. He was her only hope. "Well, fine!" she agreed reluctantly. "If you retrieve my golden ball, I'll give you what you wish!"

With the Princess's assurance, the Frog dove happily down into the murky water, coming up a few seconds later with the golden ball. He grinned and dropped it at Misty's feet.

2 3

YES!

Hey, wait for me! Remember our agreement!

I sense a lack of commitment on her part!

Me, too.

Predictably, later that night at dinner, the Royal Family heard a knock at their castle door. Princess Misty's heart sank.

How rude! Right in the middle of our family time!

Uh-oh!

Isn't someone going to get that?

I'm here! What's for dinner?!

The King and Queen were stunned. They had that familiar look on their faces when they turned toward their daughter. Princess Misty grew quiet.

Now, don't get all worked up! I had an *exciting* day . . . !

This should be good!

You bet!

Upon hearing their daughter's story, the King and Queen agreed that Princess Misty had some promises to fulfill to the helpful Frog. They urged her to make all the necessary arrangements.

Yum! Let's start with *dinner*!

Ooooh, YUCK! Have mine— I'm not hungry!

The Princess then reluctantly ordered a bed be brought for her unwanted roommate.

. . . and make it a *small* one! I don't want it to be the focal point of my room!

24

The Princess and the Pea

Princess Destiny was drenched! The weather had taken an unpredicted turn for the worse, putting a damper on her stroll.

I thought they'd said "partly cloudy," not "torrential"! Whenever I get some free time, something like this always happens! I feel so unfulfilled! Yesterday, a last minute joust to judge, and now a downpour! I need some space; new surroundings!

Sounds like a bad case of wanderlust!

Mmm, a bit of a vagabond, isn't she?

Sensing her oncoming crisis, Destiny decided to see if the local royal family could put her up for the night. She dripped, wrung, and rang the bell.

Goodness! What's this soggy, wet girl doing on our drawbridge? Is it Halloween?

Oooh! That's no ordinary soggy, wet girl, Mom! She's a *beautiful* princess! I think she might be my *future!*

No, I'm *Destiny*, not *Future*! But it's a common mistake. Have you a room for the night? I can provide references, if required. My parents are Princess Misty and Prince Todd from the next kingdom . . .

. . .Well, aren't *you* just too adorable?!

"Oh, Mom, let her stay!" urged the adorable Prince, eagerly straightening his crown. "She seems very nice! We surely have room and letting her drip will absolutely *ruin* the terra-cotta tile!"

Many thanks, Your Majesty! And don't worry, I clean up nicely!

I think you look great already!

Who's going to *clean up* that mess?

Using her finely developed powers of observation, the Queen sensed an attraction brewing. She was immediately grateful for all of her recent research on defrocking royal imposters.

We'll see how "royal" this sodden beauty really is! I can't have my boy duped by just any damsel in a tiara!

What do you think *she's* up to?

I dunno, but she's sure been reading an awful lot lately!

"Come in, my dear," beckoned the Queen graciously. "Please warm yourself by the fire."

Hmmm, curious behavior!

Oooh, central heating!

And a dry basement, too!

Doesn't anyone make introductions anymore?

Undetected, the Queen slipped away to the guest chamber. She ordered her servants to pile twenty mattresses and just as many warm quilts on the bed. On top of the bottom mattress, she placed a small pea.

I recently read in *Better Moats and Gardens,* that a *true* princess could never be comfy sleeping on top of even such a small lump as this! My brilliant idea will prove she's a phony!

I wish she'd never subscribed to that magazine! It always gives *her* crazy ideas and *us* work!

Yes! Wouldn't a call to the girl's parents be easier?

Must be a *hard* pea!

Like a rock!

Satisfied with her plan, the Queen escorted the now-dry Destiny to her room. Destiny thought the accommodations alarming.

Good night! Sleep well, my dear!

In the morning, I can show you around the castle. We've just recently redone the entire West Wing in lovely neutral shades!

I sure hope I don't roll out of bed!

In case anyone cares, I'll be up reading for a while!

Taking a running start, Destiny hoisted herself into bed, exhausted after her day's wet wanderings. She was looking forward to tomorrow's tour with that adorable Prince.

With so much padding, you'd think this bed would have fewer lumps! I'll have to ask the Prince who did their interior decorating!

For Destiny, it was a long night. She had never slept in such an uncomfortable bed, and by morning, her body ached.

At breakfast, she tried to be gracious and polite, but was a wreck from all her tossing and turning.

Good morning, Destiny. Sleep well?

Thank you, but I must admit, Your Majesty, that I've spent better nights on horseback! Don't you people know anything about comfort? Those mattresses must have been around since the Dark Ages!

Gee, you sure look lovely in the morning!

Gasp! She's really royal!

Please pass the Feudal Flakes.

Satisfied that Destiny had passed the test and proved herself a true Princess, the Queen confessed her experiment.

I hope you're not upset with me, but I had to be sure you were royal enough for my son—and not just another bewitched amphibian!

That's all right, Your Majesty. I come from a long line of sneaky skeptics myself—although your last comment *is* puzzling!

Isn't she amazing? And so understanding, too!

Hello? How about those Feudal Flakes?

On their wedding day,
there was much happiness and rejoicing in both
palaces. Each family was thrilled with their new in-laws,
and many lovely gifts were bestowed upon the happy couple.

Oh, Darwin! This
evolved into the
perfect day!

I know! It just seemed so natural
we'd select each other!

Hard to believe their families had never met!
They were
practically
neighbors!

Yes, guess they didn't get
out much!

I think
we need a
larger home—
we have so many
mattresses!

Ooon, yes!
And let's do the walls in
lovely shades
of pea green!

Hey, I've got just the
ticket! I've recently started
my own real estate business! How
about a beautiful pre-construction site in
my new development—four lovely
castle lots are available!

Well, look at you! Guess that
trip down the Career Path
did *you* a world of good!

Yes, doesn't she look well?

Indeed! And,
she seems much
happier!